Perfectly
POPPY

Football Star

Story by Michele Jakubowski

Pictures by Erica-Jane Waters

First published in the UK by Curious Fox,
an imprint of Capstone Global Library Limited,
7 Pilgrim Street, London, EC4V 6LB
Registered company number: 6695582

www.curious-fox.com

Illustrations by Erica-Jane Waters
All characters in this publication are fictitious and any resemblance to real persons,
living or dead, is purely coincidental.

ISBN: 978 1 782 02199 5
19 18 17 16 15
10 9 8 7 6 5 4 3 2 1

A CIP catalogue for this book is available from the British Library.

Image credits: Shutterstock
Designer: Kristi Carlson

Printed in China by Nordica
0914/CA21401512

Table of Contents

Chapter 1

Football Excitement

Poppy was excited. She was going to play football with her best friend, Millie. Millie had played last year and loved it.

Poppy had a lot of questions about football. Millie told Poppy how much fun it was.

"I like to score goals," Millie
said. "Everyone shouts and jumps
up and down."

"I can't wait to get my football kit," Poppy said.

She remembered Millie's kit from last year. It was so cool!

"Before each game we get in a
huddle and do a cheer," Millie said.

"I love to cheer," said Poppy.

"And after the game we get snacks," Millie said. "You are going to love it!"

"I sure am!" Poppy said. She couldn't wait to play football.

"Practice starts tomorrow," Millie said. "Don't be late."

"I'm too excited to be late," Poppy said.

Chapter 2

Practise, Practise, Practise

Poppy and Millie had football practice twice a week. They had been practising for over two weeks now. Poppy frowned as her mum drove her to another practice.

Poppy was in a bad mood. She had been having fun playing with her dolls when her mum said it was time to go. She didn't want to stop playing to go to another football practice.

When they got to the football field, Poppy joined her team for stretches. As she reached over to touch her toes, Poppy lost her balance and fell over.

Next each player took turns dribbling the ball down to a cone and back.

When it was Poppy's turn, she had a hard time. First she kicked the ball too hard. She had to chase it across the field. Then she kicked it too softly. She almost tripped over it. Poppy was very frustrated!

Poppy's coach helped her with
her kicks. She tried again and
again. Poppy got better each time,
but she wasn't having fun. She
was happy when the coach said
practice was over.

"See you at the game tomorrow morning," he said.

"Aren't you excited about the game?" Millie asked.

"I guess," Poppy said.

"What's wrong?" Millie asked.

"I'm not sure football is for me," Poppy said.

"Just wait until the game tomorrow. All this practise will be worth it," Millie said.

"Promise?" Poppy asked.

"Pinky promise," Millie said.

Chapter 3
Game Day

Poppy woke up feeling nervous. Putting on her new kit helped. The shirt was green, which was Poppy's favourite colour. Poppy's mum pulled her hair back using a bright green ribbon. It was perfect.

Poppy was feeling better as her team did stretches. She reached over and touched her toes with no problem. She dribbled the ball to the cone and back with no problem.

The girls huddled together for
a big cheer to start the game. By
half-time, Poppy was having a
great time.

After half-time, Poppy and Millie were playing on the field at the same time. Millie was very good. She got the ball and headed for the goal. When someone from the other team tried to take the ball, she kicked it to Poppy.

Poppy started dribbling down the field. She tried to remember what the coach had taught her. She was glad she had practised so much.

Poppy saw a player from the other team coming for her. She quickly kicked the ball back to Millie. Millie pulled her leg back and kicked the ball. It went into the net! Goal!

Everyone cheered! Poppy and Millie hugged each other and jumped up and down. All their hard work had paid off.

"Is it snack time now?" Poppy asked.

"It sure is," Millie said.

"I guess football *is* for me," Poppy said as she ate her fruit and nut mix.

"You are a football star," Millie said, smiling.

Poppy's Diary

Dear Diary,

Millie scored an amazing goal at the football game today!

Practising is hard and it didn't feel worth it at first. But I didn't feel as nervous when we started playing. When I remembered what I'd been taught, I felt proud. Practising was worth it after all!

Now I feel brave about trying more new things! Maybe I'll try netball or hockey next?

Poppy

Football Snacks

Playing football is a lot of work. After every game we get a healthy snack to boost our energy. Eating is almost as fun as playing! Remember to ask if anyone on your team has any allergies. Then grab your water bottle, find a shady spot to relax and enjoy your snack.

- Small sandwiches (with fillings such as peanut butter, ham, turkey) on wholewheat bread

- Cheese and apples or pears

- Homemade snack mix made of things like popcorn, raisins, peanuts, almonds, chocolate chips and cereal

- Fruit kebab with pineapple, grapes and cheese

- Veggies and hummus dip

- Banana or apple muffins

- Tubes of frozen yogurt

Perfectly POPPY

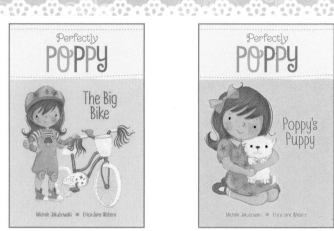

The Big Bike £3.99
9781782022008

Poppy's Puppy £3.99
9781782021988

Football Star £3.99
9781782021995

Outside Surprise £3.99
9781782022015

Read all of Poppy's adventures!
Available from all good booksellers.